To Dad, for everything
C. S.

For Larisa
F. L.

AUTHOR'S NOTE

The story of Pattan is told by the Irula people who live
in the hills of Mannarkadu in the Palakkad district of Kerala,
in southern India. They view themselves as descendants
of Pattan. I first read the story in Philipose Vaidyar's book
A Peep into the Tribalscape, in which he says it was told to
him by an Irula villager. In the original story, Pattan and
his family travel in a *churraka,* a bottle gourd, one of the
earliest fruits cultivated by mankind. I have translated this
as pumpkin, which is a similar but more familiar fruit.

First U.S. edition 2017

Library of Congress Catalog Card Number pending
ISBN 978-0-7636-9274-2

16 17 18 19 20 21 APS 10 9 8 7 6 5 4 3 2 1

Printed in Humen, Dongguan, China

This book was typeset in Bell Gothic.
The illustrations were done in gouache.

Candlewick Press
99 Dover Street
Somerville, Massachusetts 02144

visit us at www.candlewick.com

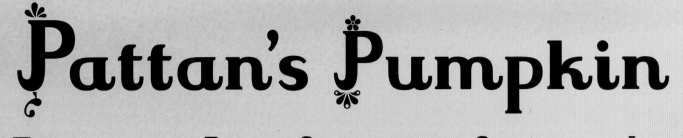

Pattan's Pumpkin

A Traditional Flood Story from Southern India

Chitra Soundar

illustrated by Frané Lessac

CANDLEWICK PRESS

Once upon a time, there was a man named Pattan.
He lived with his wife, Kanni, on the banks of
a mighty river that galloped down the Sahyadri Mountains.
They tended their goats, fed their bulls,
and rode the elephants that roamed their lands.

Pattan grew pepper, rice, nutmeg, and bananas.
He shared his food with everyone — the animals,
the birds, and the insects.

One day, Pattan found an ailing plant in the valley.

It had beautiful yellow flowers.

I'll plant it by my hut and look after it, he thought.

The plant liked its new home.
Its yellow flowers smiled at the sun.
"Look!" Pattan called one day.
"A pumpkin has started to grow."

The pumpkin grew a little every day.
"It's taller than the goats now,"
said Kanni.

The pumpkin had grown
taller than the fence, too.
It was even fatter than the pigs.

It grew some more.
Pattan had to climb on an elephant to see the top of the pumpkin.

And still it grew bigger . . . and bigger . . .
and **BIGGER.**

"Soon it will be as tall as the mountain," said Pattan.

The next day, dark clouds gathered. Rain crashed against the rocks in fury. Pattan was afraid that the floods would wash away his hut.

"We should leave the mountains tomorrow," he said. "We should take all the animals, birds, beetles, and bugs with us. And a sapling of every plant and seeds of every grain."

But how were they going to take all the creatures
with them?

Pattan couldn't sleep that night. When the pumpkin
glowed like fire under a burst of lightning,
he had an idea. . . .

In the morning, Pattan reached for his ax.

"It's time to harvest the pumpkin," he said.

Battling the lashing rain, Pattan climbed the mountain.

The birds and animals followed him.

Then Pattan jumped on top of the pumpkin.

He cut a big hole in it and dived into its orange flesh.

The birds called out in fear.

The goats bleated.

The bulls **snorted**.

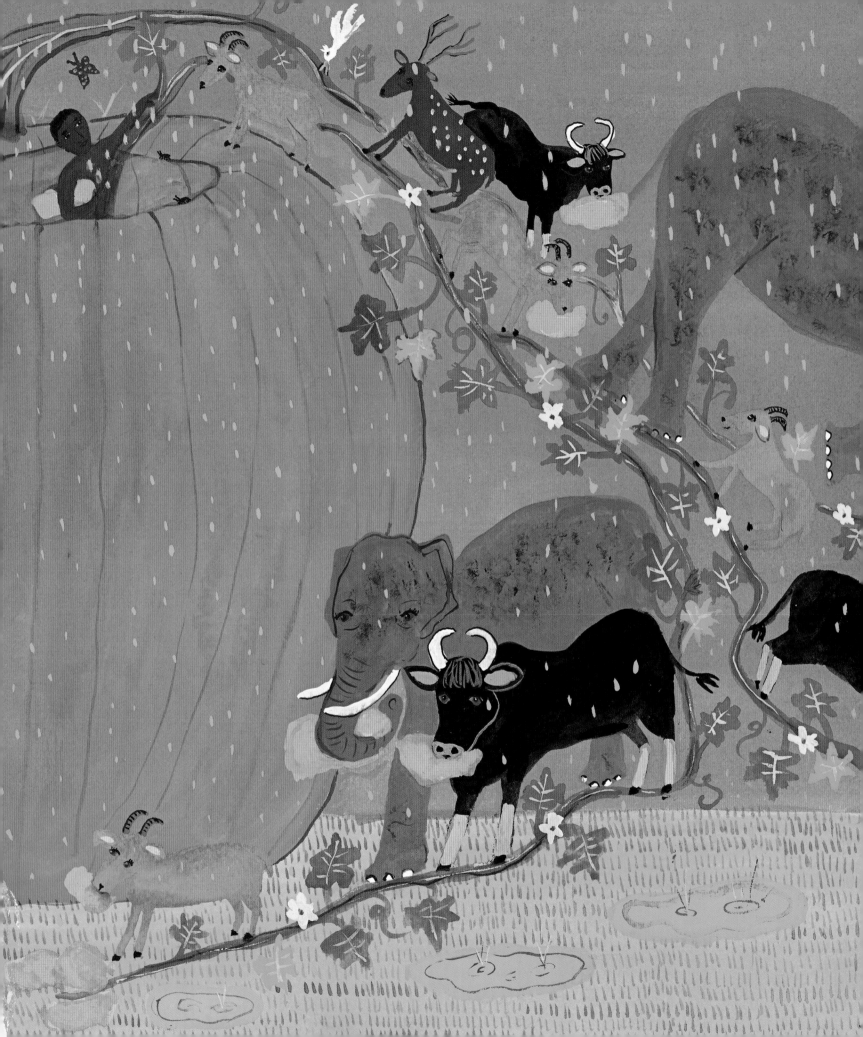

Pattan dug into the pumpkin, hollowing out its insides.
"Help me!" he called.
The goats, the bulls, and the birds ferried out
the pumpkin flesh as fast as they could.

The wind blew hard, rocking the pumpkin from
side to side. But Pattan did not give up.
He dug and dug until the pumpkin was hollow.

At last it was **BIG** enough inside for everyone.

Down in the valley, Kanni filled sacks with grain, seeds, and herbs. Pattan loaded them onto the goats, elephants, and bulls and brought them up the mountainside.

"Hurry — climb in!" Pattan cried.

The dark evening skies cradled the mountain in darkness.

"We must leave before nightfall," said Pattan,

cutting the prickly stem from the plant.

Now the pumpkin was **FREE**.

It **rolled** down the mountain and **bounced**
into the river. The crested waters of the river
carried the pumpkin along.

Many a day and night must have passed.
No one counted.
It rained . . .

and rained . . .

and rained.

Kanni sang a lullaby to soothe the baby animals and birds.

"While the gods of rain and thunder send us a storm,
Here inside the pumpkin we are safe and warm.
One day we will return to our mountain peak,
But in this great darkness, light is what we seek."

And then, one day, the pumpkin bumped against something and **stopped**.

Pattan climbed out into a bright and sunny day.
"We've reached the plains!" he called joyfully.
Kanni and all the creatures hurried out.
The troubles of the rain were finally over.

"The pumpkin has saved us,"
said Kanni.

The animals and birds basked
in the sunshine.

The next morning, Pattan gathered everyone together.
"It's time to return home," he said.

Back in the valley, they built a new house by the river.
"I'm forever grateful to the pumpkin," Pattan said,
as he planted the single pumpkin seed he had saved.

Pattan and Kanni had many children,
and they all made their homes in the
foothills of the Sahyadri Mountains.

Even today, Pattan's descendants live in this valley,
looking after their animals and growing pumpkins.
They remember Pattan and Kanni
with reverence and love.